Second Grade Costume Parade

STORY BY
Tasha N. Smith

ILLUSTRATIONS BY
HATICE BAYRAMOGLU

LPP Publishing™

Second Grade Costume Parade

For information about special discounts for bulk purchases, please contact

Little Pink Princess LLC at:

LittlePinkPrincess.LLC@Gmail.com

First Edition 1 2 3 4 5 6 7 8 9 10

ISBN 978-1-7332643-3-4

This book is dedicated to:

My "Little Pink Princess":

Aria Faith Smith

And her wonderful Parents:

Chris & Shannon

Thank you for sharing your "miracle girl" with me and the world!

Mrs. Conrad stood in front of the class and cleared her throat. That's what she did when she wanted to make an announcement. The students settled down and waited to hear what Mrs. Conrad had to say. "Class, I want to remind you that the costume parade is in three days" she said, and pointed to the calendar with a big red circle around October 31st.

Maya and her friends clapped and cheered. Everyone was super excited about Halloween and the school costume parade.

At lunch, Mason stood up and said, "I'm going to be a Chef for Halloween. I already have the jacket and the hat."

Mason wanted to be a famous chef and have a cooking show on TV. He always made delicious treats and shared them with the class.

"Well I'm going to be a ladybug" said Susan as she twirled around and

flapped her arms like they were wings.

In gym class, Jordan held a bat and said, "I'm going to be a baseball player for Halloween."

Maya loved baseball, and she thought about dressing up as a player for Halloween too. But after giving it a lot of thought, she chose a different costume, and hoped it would be special enough for second grade.

"What are you going to be for Halloween?" Maya asked Angel at the water fountain.

"My family doesn't celebrate Halloween," Angel answered. "But my parents said I can dress up for the costume parade, so I'm going to be a teacher – like Mrs. Conrad," she said with a big smile

On the bus ride home Susan asked "Did you decide on a costume Maya?"

"Yes" Maya replied. "I'm going to be a pumpkin."

"A Pumpkin?" Mason said with a puzzled look on his face.

"Yes, a pumpkin. I'm going to be a pumpkin" Maya repeated.

Maya could hardly wait for five o'clock. She loved when her cousin Joanne came over.

Her Mom always made them special things to eat.

Tonight they would be having Joanne's favorite - meatball sub sandwiches, and Maya's favorite – iced oatmeal cookies.

Halfway through pumpkin decorating Joanne stood up and said, "I'm going to be a Little Pink Princess for Halloween. What are you going to be Maya?"

"I'm going to be a pumpkin," Maya said. She looked at Joanne and saw a frown on her face.

"Why do you want to be a pumpkin?" Joanne asked.

"I just do!" Maya said

Maya's mother came into her bedroom, holding up her pumpkin costume.

"It's perfect" Maya said as she ran her fingers over the soft material.

"I'm glad you like it", said her mother. "Let's try it on and go show your

father."

Maya's mother helped her into the costume, then they walked out into the

family room.

"Wow… look at my little pumpkin" Maya's dad said with a big smile.

"Really? Do you mean it?" Maya asked.

"Of course I do. Why would that change?" asked her father.

"Well… because I'm a big girl now. I'm in the second grade! And I don't know if a BIG girl in the second grade can still be a LITTLE pumpkin. I really like being your little pumpkin… that's why I chose this costume" Maya said.

Maya's father picked her up and sat her on his lap.

"No matter what grade you're in, no matter how big you get, even when you're old enough to get married and have a little pumpkin of your own – you will forever, and for always be MY little pumpkin" he said, and gave her a soft peck on the top of her pumpkin hat.

Maya was very excited to hear her father say that. She gave him a tight squeeze around the neck and squealed "forever and for always!" then she jumped down and ran to get ready for bed. She was eager to get to school the next day and show off her very special costume.

"Everyone looks amazing," Mrs. Conrad sang as she went around the class taking pictures.

"It's officially time for the 2nd grade costume parade! Since its Mason's day to be the line leader, everyone will follow him."

"Mrs. Conrad", Mason said raising his hand, "I would like to give my line leader position to Maya today, because I think she has the best costume." Maya's friends cheered in agreement.

"I think that's a good idea," said Mrs. Conrad, while motioning for the kids to get in line. Maya stood up straight and tall, and took her place as the line leader. She ran her fingers over the soft material of her costume again and smiled. Today, she was indeed a Big Girl in the second grade, but she was also still her father's Little Pumpkin and that made her very happy. Mrs. Conrad opened the classroom door and gave the start signal. As Maya began leading her friends down the hallway, she knew this was going to be a very special Halloween and a great costume parade.

Made in the USA
Las Vegas, NV
28 September 2021